Lazarus

The girl was sitting so quietly I had not noticed her.

Her long black hair was braided and shiny. She wore a calico dress sewn with bright-colored beads. Her dark eyes watched me as I walked toward her.

"What is your name?" she asked.

"Libby," I said. "What's yours?"

"I am called Taw cum e go qua and I am of the clan of the eagle." Fastened around her neck was a piece of rawhide holding a tiny silver eagle.

For Jacqueline

Text copyright © 1987 by Gloria Whelan.
Text illustrations copyright © 1987 by Random House, Inc.
Cover illustration copyright © 1997 by Tony Meers.

http://www.randomhouse.com/

Library of Congress Cataloging-in-Publication Data
Whelan, Gloria. Next spring an oriole. (A Stepping stone book)
   p. cm.   SUMMARY: In 1837 ten-year-old Libby and her parents journey by
covered wagon to the Michigan frontier, where they make themselves a new home
near friendly Indians and other pioneers.
ISBN: 0-394-89125-2 (pbk.) — 0-394-99125-7 (lib. bdg.)
[1. Frontier and pioneer life—Michigan—Fiction. 2. Michigan—Fiction.
3. Indians of North America—Fiction.] I. Johnson, Pamela, ill. II. Title. III. Series.
PZ7.W5718Ne 1987 [E] 87-4910

Printed in the United States of America 20 19

Next Spring an Oriole

by Gloria Whelan

illustrated by Pamela Johnson

cover illustration by Tony Meers

A STEPPING STONE BOOK

Random House New York

I

My name is Elizabeth Mitchell. I am called Libby. On my tenth birthday, April 3, 1837, my mama and papa and I left the state of Virginia and everyone we loved. That was two months ago. Since then we have come a thousand miles through woods and swamps.

Mama is from the Tidewater country and grew up in a big house with pretty things, while Papa is a surveyor from north Virginia. Mama loves the town but Papa loves the trees. When our neighbors cut down all their trees for a plantation, Papa said he was ready to leave.

Then a land-looker came by with stories about the state of Michigan, where you could buy an acre of land for $1.25. He said pine trees there were so tall you couldn't see their tops unless you lay down on the ground. Papa went out and bought a wagon. When he brought it home, Mama cried.

I am more like Papa. Although I was sorry to leave my friends, I was glad to put away the dresses that pinched my waist and the shoes that pinched my toes. Instead of walking two miles each way to school, where the schoolmaster, Mr. Ripple, slapped our fingers with a ruler when we didn't have our lesson by heart, Mama would teach me reading, writing, and sums. And each day there would be something to see that I had never seen before.

It was early spring when we left Virginia. I could hear orioles and thrushes for the first time since the winter. I would rather hear an oriole sing than anything else in the world. The oriole is beautiful to look at, too, with its flash of orange that turns to gold in the sun.

The wagon we traveled in was about three

times as big as my parents' bed. It had
rounded bows stretched over the top. The
bows were covered with canvas. Our horses,
Ned and Dan, pulled the wagon. We could

take along only what would fit in the wagon and still leave room for us to make up a bed at night. Papa took his axe, his musket, and his surveying tools. I took my doll with the face Mama had painted to look just like me. Mama took the most precious things she owned—her sketchbook and pencils. We also took salt pork, corn, dried apples, a skillet, and an iron kettle.

After the two months of travel our wagon pulled into Detroit. We saw real houses made of brick and women wearing fashionable dresses. While we rode through the town I looked hard at everything to make it last. There were children playing games. There were Indians with piles of animal skins. There were stores with barrels of flour and molasses and lengths of bright-colored cloth. There were hotels with people sitting on the porches and there were ships sailing on the river. In a few hours I knew it would all be gone and we would be back in the woods, woods deeper than any we had traveled through before.

When Papa stopped the wagon at the land office, Mama got out her sketchbook and began to draw the boats. She made quick marks, like bird wings, for the sails; as though the boats could fly through the air as well as sail on the water.

Papa went into the land office to get the deed to our property. When he came out, a man walked over to the wagon to ask him where we were going. "We're taking the Saginaw Trail," Papa said.

The man shook his head until I was afraid his top hat would fall off. "Why, there's nothing there but trees," he said. "You should settle in Pontiac. A lot of that land has been cleared."

"It's the trees I'm after," Papa told him.

Later Mama asked, "Rob, that man sounded as though he believed we were daft. How do we know that the land-looker was telling us the truth?"

Papa showed her his bill of sale. "Eighty acres for one hundred dollars, Vinnie. And why should we go somewhere where everything is already done? I'd rather have a hand in it."

Because it was June it stayed light a long time, so we were able to drive the wagon halfway to Pontiac. Papa said we were making nearly two miles an hour. We camped in a kind of meadow Papa called an oak clearing.

While Papa was making the campfire and Mama was mixing corn cakes, I went off a little way, but not so far that I couldn't see the wagon. Nighthawks were dropping out of the sky to catch the mosquitoes. The birds fell almost to the ground and then jerked themselves up as though someone were pulling them on strings. I looked down at my bare feet and saw that they were all red and sticky. At first I was scared, thinking it was blood, but when I looked closer I saw I had been walking in a field of wild strawberries. I hadn't tasted fresh fruit since we left Virginia. I called to Mama and Papa. In a minute we were all down on our hands and knees picking the tiny sweet berries.

There was still a little light left in the sky

when I had to climb into the wagon and go to sleep. Mama was sitting by the fire talking with Papa. She was unpinning her long hair, which fell to her waist and was the color of Virginia wheat fields. My hair is dark like Papa's. I hope someday it will be as long as Mama's; now it just comes to my shoulders.

Even though Mama and Papa were talking to each other and not paying me any attention, I didn't feel lonesome. I was excited. Our long journey was almost over.

II

After we left Pontiac, the road led through a thick woods. Papa was pleased because there were so many trees. We startled deer and made the squirrels scold from the branches. Late in the morning it began to rain. Mama and I climbed into the back of the wagon. Papa put on his oiled leather jacket and big hat.

The rain was everywhere. It poured off the brim of Papa's hat so that he could hardly see. It lay in puddles on the top of the wagon's canvas roof. If we brushed against the canvas, water dripped into the wagon. The rain slid down the backs of Ned and Dan and got into their ears so that they flicked them and shook their heads.

The trail became soft and squishy. The wagon wheels sunk deeper and deeper. Papa jumped down from the wagon so it would be lighter. He pulled on the horses' bridles and coaxed them along. After a little while Mama climbed down and walked alongside Papa. In minutes her dress and shawl were soaked through. Her wet skirt clung to her legs, and its hem was scalloped with mud.

We came to a long hill so slick with mud that Papa had to tie a dead tree to the wagon. He and Mama climbed back into the wagon so it would be heavy and wouldn't go sliding down the slippery hill. Ned and Dan kept pulling. They were tired and moving slowly, and their hoofs made an awful sucking sound each time they pulled them out of the mud.

At the bottom of the hill we found a stream. The rain was letting up and we all got out of the wagon to see how deep the water was. Then the sun came out; a hot June sun. The banks on either side of the river began to steam with heat. Papa threw off his hat and jacket. "The river is swollen from the rain," he said. "We'd better camp here. In the morning the water will be lower and we'll make it across." He looked at Mama, whose clothes and face and hair were plastered with mud. Papa began to laugh. Mama looked angry for a minute. Then she laughed too.

"You look just as bad as I do, Rob Mitchell, and it's time you had a bath." With that she pushed him into the river and then waded in herself. In a minute I jumped in too. We splashed one another and scrubbed off the mud and washed our clothes. When we were clean, we waded out of the stream and lay down on the grass. Mama had washed her hair and spread it out in the sun to dry. When I touched it, it was so warm from the sun it seemed almost alive.

Papa led Ned and Dan down to the riverbank and sloshed them with pails of water. While Papa was washing down the horses, Mama got out her sketchbook and drew Papa's picture. I like to watch her draw. She catches her lower lip between her teeth and frowns a little, and she always finds more to put in her picture than I can see. I was watching Papa sluice down the horses, but I hadn't seen the fond look he gave them or the gentleness in his hands. All that was in Mama's drawing.

In the morning the river was down and we forded the stream easily. Once on the other side, the trail gave out. It looked like we could go one way as well as another. Papa shook his head. "You and Libby stay with the wagon," he told Mama, "and I'll ride Ned a little way into the woods and see where these trails lead." He took his musket with him. "I'll find us some partridge for dinner," he promised.

When Papa came riding back, an Indian was walking alongside him. We had seen Indians on our trip and they had done us no harm, but I had never been so close to one. This man had on deerskin trousers, leggings, and a long shirt. On his feet were moccasins. His long black hair, all but a few locks, hung down his back. The few locks were coiled into a little heap on the top of his head and were stuck through with feathers. He carried a musket like Papa's.

"Vinnie," said Papa, "this man is a Potawatomi. He and his family are camped near here. They were on their way to Saginaw to sell some skins to the fur company, but their daughter is very ill and they can't travel until she is better."

"What's wrong with her?" Mama asked.

"She has measles," Papa said. He turned to me. "You remember, Libby, when you had them two years ago. We had a hard time keeping you in bed. But when the Indians get measles it is much more serious. The little girl looks feverish."

"Rob, tell them we will take the child in our wagon. She can rest on our bed and I can nurse her."

Papa and the Indian were soon back. Between them they carried a kind of movable bed made of two long poles and strips of birch bark. On the cot was the Indian girl, and walking along behind her was an Indian woman and a small boy. Papa carried the girl into our wagon and laid her down gently. She was a little older than I. Her long black hair lay spread over the pillow. She wore a plain shift that came to her knees. She was moaning softly and seemed barely able to open her eyes. When she saw us standing over her, she looked frightened, as though, were she able, she would surely run away.

"We must do something about her fever," Mama said. She bathed the girl with cool water and brewed some tea from sage leaves for her. The girl slept most of the afternoon. Mama said as long as I was quiet I might sit near the bed. In spite of the red measles on her face, I thought the Indian girl so pretty I couldn't take my eyes from her. I was happy to know, too, that somewhere in the woods there was a girl nearly my age.

At dinnertime the girl drank a little broth Mama made for her from a partridge Papa had shot. We shared our dinner with the girl's mama and papa and little brother, but they would not sit by the fire with us. Instead, they carried their partridge and corn cakes a little way off from the wagon. While they ate they never took their eyes from us. This made us uneasy. "They seem not to trust us, Rob," Mama said.

"They have little reason to. First the white man buys the Indians' land for a pittance, and now I hear tell they want to round up all the Potawatomis and take them west of the Mississippi."

That night the Indians slept under the trees, wrapped in their blankets to protect them from the mosquitoes.

The girl was better in the morning, and it was decided that she could rest in the wagon while we continued on our way. The Indians followed along, keeping a little distance between themselves and the wagon, but never letting us out of their sight.

The girl's eyes were open now and she watched everything we did. I wanted to try to talk with her but Mama said she must rest, and anyhow, she probably would not understand me. At this I saw the girl's eyes open a little wider, but she said nothing. She drank the tea and broth Mama fixed for her and even took the medicine she was given without a murmur. When I had the measles and had to take it, I complained loudly that it was bitter and bad tasting.

The next day the Indian girl was well enough to return to her family. Had it been our family, there would have been much hugging and joyful words when we were reunited. The Indians took back their daughter in silence.

The Potawatomis led us to a narrow trail and, indicating the direction we were to take, left us without once looking back. We were only a short time on the road when we came to a stand of trees whose very newest leaves were brown and withered. Papa showed me circles that had been cut into the bark of all the trunks. "They girdle the trees," he said, "so the leaves die. Then they have enough sunlight to grow a crop." We could see where the ground had been plowed, the furrows winding in and out of the trees. "I suppose the farmers must clear the land if they are to eat, but I hate to see a sight like this, for the trees are wasted."

Moments later we saw a cabin. There were no windows in the cabin, but a man stood in the doorway. He was the largest, fattest man

I have ever seen. He looked us up and down, and then he said, "Welcome to Saginaw, the end of the world, and the Lord have mercy upon you."

III

The man was most friendly to us and told us his name was Herbert LaBelle. He had a funny way of saying his words. Mama said he was a Frenchman. I couldn't help staring at him. On his head he wore a fur hat that Papa said was mink, and over his prodigious body he wore a great cape so that he looked like a small mountain. His wife came to welcome us. A friendly woman, as thin as her husband was fat, she was attended by several small children dressed in ragged clothes. The children's faces were dirty and their hair was cut so short it stood up on their heads like the quills of a porcupine.

As the LaBelles were leading us toward

their cabin we heard a great stirring and rumbling. In the twilight we could make out the shape of a huge animal tethered to a stake. The beast reared up and I hid behind Papa.

Mr. LaBelle said, "Don't mind him. It's just our bear, Voltaire. We keep him for a watchdog. Mind you don't get too close. He's not particular if his supper is cooked or uncooked or if it walks on four legs or two."

Mrs. LaBelle urged us into their cabin, and as graciously as if they had been fine chairs, pulled up some tree stumps for us to sit upon. There was only a dirt floor and it was not well swept. Bedclothes were piled here and there, and the walls were covered with all kinds of dried animal skins. Wooden dishes were scattered over a long plank that served as a table. There were no candles, only long strips of pork fat coiled into a tin cup. Sizzling and splattering as it burned, it gave hardly any light. There was very little food on the table, but Mrs. LaBelle and her husband hastened to share it with us.

The many little children tumbled over one another to assist their mother. They must not have seen many visitors, for they crept close to us, staring up at Mama and Papa and me and touching our clothes. They took after their father with their chubby little bodies and round faces. Their short haircuts and strange clothes made it difficult to tell which were girls and which were boys, but after a while I sorted them out into three little girls and two boys.

"I hope you don't mean to make a living by farming, sir," Mr. LaBelle said to Papa. "It will take a good while before you can clear enough land to support your family. If I did not have my animal skins to sell, we would have starved long ago."

Papa said, "I had hoped in a new settlement like this there would be a need for a surveyor. That is my trade and I hope to make my living at it."

"There are few families here now," Mr. LaBelle said, "but more come each month, and once a year the boat steams up the river from Lake Huron with settlers. Why shouldn't you find a use for your trade? Roger, stop that!" None of the children wore shoes, and one little boy had removed mine. After examining them carefully, he was trying to walk in them.

When we had finished eating, Mr. LaBelle

urged us to spend the night in their cabin. It was drizzling outside and the thought of how damp and cold our beds in the wagon would be persuaded us. The best bedclothes, though none too clean, were laid out for us in one corner of the cabin. The children, who looked as if they were ready to climb into bed with us, were shooed to the opposite side.

"Your wagon will come to no harm with Voltaire to watch over it," Mr. LaBelle told Papa. "In the morning you can find your property. I must warn you, you will need the safety of your own cabin as soon as possible. There are trappers here who have not taken kindly to settlers coming. They don't want the land cleared and the swamps drained, for the fox and the mink and all the other wild animals will then go elsewhere."

Papa said, "They will find me less an enemy than they think. I left our home in Virginia because men were too eager to turn every good thing God created to their own use."

Soon we were all in our corners, wrapped in the LaBelles' quilts. I was so tired from the

long journey, I slept soundly in spite of Mr.
LaBelle's great snores and the mouselike scur-
ryings and rustlings of the children as they
shifted about among themselves on their
straw mattress.

When I awoke it was morning, and Mama was sitting straight up, whispering to Papa. She was trying to hide some worry that had come upon her in the night. In a minute she had her shoes laced and was making apologies to the LaBelles. "You have been so generous. We can't impose further on your hospitality. Mr. Mitchell is anxious to see our land, and if you will excuse us, we will be on our way." Mama said all that very nicely, but I could tell she was upset.

Voltaire growled and pulled at his chain. Mr. and Mrs. LaBelle stood at their doorway and waved. The children scrambled onto our wagon and had to be dragged away. "As soon as we have a cabin you must come to visit us," called Mama.

"We will do better than that," answered Mr. LaBelle. "We will help you to build the cabin."

At this, the children cheered up and loosened their hold on the wagon, and the horses started up.

Once we were out of sight of the house and into the woods, Mama began to sob. Papa stopped the horses and tried to comfort her. "They'll go away," he said.

"What will go away?" I asked, looking around.

Mama turned to me. "Do you feel nothing on your head? I pray to the Lord you have escaped, Libby."

"Nothing," I said. "Only little pinpricks." Now that I thought about it, there was a funny feeling all through my hair, as if something were running about in it on tiny tiptoes.

"You, too!" Mama said, and cried louder than ever. "I should have thought of lice when I saw those children with their hair all cut off."

"Oh, Mama! I won't have to cut my hair like that! I don't want it to stick up all over my head."

Mama was a little calmer. "No, but we shall have to cut it or we will never get rid of the lice."

"Not your hair, Mama. You won't cut your hair!"

"Yes," she said. "I will." She went into the back, searching for the scissors. When she found them, she climbed down. "Now, then," she said. She sounded very brave, but her face was streaked with tears. She unpinned her long hair that had taken years and years to grow and with a few snips cut it as short as Papa's, so that it just covered her ears. Then she did a funny thing. She took her lovely long silky hair that had been cut off and went scattering it under the trees and hanging it on the branches.

"What are you doing?" I asked.

"It will make a nice lining for the nests of the mice and birds. I don't want it wasted."

"Can I do that too?" Mama promised I could, so I let her cut mine off as short as hers. While she was busy cutting my hair, I saw Papa sneak a lock of Mama's hair from one of the branches and carefully put it into his pocket. All he said, though, when Mama had finished with me, was that we both looked younger and prettier than before and that our new short hair would set a fashion.

"I'm afraid we have left such things as fashion far behind us, Rob," Mama said. "I only hope we shall not end up with a bear chained to our doorstep and the stumps of trees to sit upon."

"They were good people, Vinnie."

"I don't say they weren't, Rob. They were kindness itself, but I am afraid we have come too far and left too much behind us."

IV

On the way to our land we passed five or six cabins. Some of the families hurried to greet us, asking where we had come from and where we were headed. They were friendly and eager to give advice and offer help. There were also cabins where men watched us pass with no word of greeting. Around those cabins there was no clearing for the planting of crops. We took those men for trappers.

Papa was so eager to find our land, it was all he could do to make his manners to those along the way. Papa urged Ned and Dan along until the wagon was bouncing so hard Mama said, "Rob, if you don't slow down every bone in my body will be shaken loose."

I was glad to hear her complain because she had been so quiet, which wasn't like Mama. Papa slowed down, but only a little. The trail narrowed and there was just enough space between the trees for the wagon. Suddenly Papa shouted, "There's the pond!" He jumped down and began to stride back and forth until at last he called, "Here's the survey stake! This is our land, Vinnie! We have the whole east shore of the pond." Papa had said nothing about the pond, wanting to surprise Mama and me. The three of us stood by the blue circle of water. After all the miles of hot, dusty trail, it was like a gift someone gives you when there is no reason for it.

Papa named everything for us as if he had just made up the names brand new—oak, popple, elm, maple, birch, hemlock, and, everywhere you looked, pine trees that nearly covered the sky. Papa was so pleased with the trees I thought he would surely put his arms around them and hug each one.

I ran down to the pond's edge. With little

slapping noises green frogs hopped into the water. A string of ducklings swam behind their mother. Down the shore a way a huge bird, nearly as tall as I was, spread its wings and slowly followed the circle of the pond to the opposite shore. "A heron," Papa said. "I'll teach you to fish, Libby, just like he's doing, and you can keep our skillet filled."

"Look over there," Mama whispered. Near where the heron had settled, a deer stood for just a moment before it moved back into the woods. "You were right, Rob," Mama said. "It's going to be a wonderful place."

But the next day and for three days more it rained. Papa was up each morning at sunrise cutting trees for a cabin. We heard the sound of his axe all day long. In the wagon Mama made sketches of the pond and trees and of Papa swinging his axe. I did my lessons and sewed patches on my petticoats.

When Mama and I couldn't stand being in the wagon for another minute, we went out into the rain to help Papa clear away the great pile of branches he had trimmed from the logs. We were always hungry because you couldn't keep a fire going in the rain. Our clothes were damp and our beds at night were as cold and clammy as the little green frogs.

By the time the rain finally stopped, Papa had cut so many logs I could close my eyes and almost see what the cabin would look like. The sun shone bright and warm into the clearing made by the felled trees. Mama took the hoe and turned up the ground. I pulled up the clumps of sod. The dirt was dark and rich, and when we buried the seed potatoes in their little hills of earth, I felt they would be happy there.

That evening Papa called to Mama and me and said we were ready to decide just where the cabin would stand. "Right on the shore of the pond," I said. "Then we can see the heron feeding and deer come down to drink."

"If you put it at the edge of the pond," Papa said, "there will be no trees to protect us, and in the winter, wind and snow will blow across the pond. It would be better to set the cabin among the trees. They will shelter us from the northwest winds."

"But it's so dark in the trees," Mama said.

"I'll put one window on the east side for the morning sun and one window on the west side for the afternoon sun. If I cut down a tree or two in front of the windows there will be light enough."

Papa took a sharp stick and drew a big square on the ground, about twice as big as our wagon.

"Can we sleep in our cabin tonight?" I asked.

Mama and Papa looked at me. "There is no cabin," Papa said.

I pointed to the outline Papa had made

with his stick. It was July and the night was warm. "Why couldn't we take our quilts outside and sleep right here? We could pretend the cabin was all built."

Mama and Papa exchanged looks. "Very well," Papa said. "We will. On which side of the cabin are you going to choose to sleep?" he asked me.

"On the east side," I said, "so the sun will wake me first thing in the morning."

V

On the day of our house-raising bee when the neighbors were to help us build our cabin, we got up so early it was still dark out.

"Rob, do you really believe they will come?" Mama asked.

"Mr. LaBelle gave his word," Papa said. "He's a funny fellow, but an honest one, I believe."

It was hard to imagine that by nightfall all the logs that lay scattered about would be a house.

The LaBelles were the first to arrive. The children jumped down out of the wagon and were everywhere at once. They ran down to see the pond, scrambled over the logs, climbed into our wagon to see what there might be to eat and tasted what they found.

Soon other wagons arrived. One family came a distance of twenty miles. The Indian whose daughter we had cared for came to help. "You go to a lot of trouble to build your house," he told Papa. "We make our houses from a few sticks and some birch bark. When it is time for us to move on, we are not sorry to leave. But you could not leave a house like this one without looking back many times." I wondered if he thought us foolish.

When the first logs had been laid, Mr. LaBelle, the most skillful man with an axe, was asked to be the corner man. He was the one to chop a notch at the ends of each log so they would fit one upon another. When the cabin grew to be as high as Papa's chest it became too hard to lift the logs. The men set long poles at an angle from the top log to the ground, making a kind of slide. Then they shoved and shouldered the logs up the slide and into place.

This was hard work and they were loud in

encouraging one another, sometimes saying words Mama thought it best I not hear, for she called me away to help prepare lunch. After we had all eaten, Mama pointed in the direction of the trees and said, "I believe that is the little Indian girl who had the measles. She has been too shy to eat with us, and her father has not seen to her. Take some of these corn cakes over to her, Libby."

The girl was sitting so quietly I had not noticed her. Her long black hair was braided now, and shiny. She wore a calico dress sewn with bright-colored beads. Her dark eyes watched me as I walked toward her.

I handed her the plate of corn cakes and maple syrup and made some signs of eating, believing she would not understand English.

She took the cakes and said in very good English, "Corn cakes are good, but when we have a celebration we have better food— beaver tail and the hind feet of a bear."

"Where did you learn English?" I asked, very surprised.

"When we lived a day's journey from

Detroit, I went to a school for Indians. The missionaries taught me English."

"Why did you leave there?"

"Our chiefs sold our land. Now the government agents want to send us far away from our homes. If they catch us, they will make us leave." She looked about her as though someone who meant her harm might be in the woods. After a moment she asked, "What is your name?"

"Libby. What's yours?"

"Your name is not much. I am called Taw cum e go qua and I am of the clan of the eagle." Fastened around her neck was a piece of rawhide holding a tiny silver eagle.

"Where did you get that?" I asked.

"The English gave it to my father for some skins," she said. "They give better gifts than your countrymen."

The LaBelle children had seen us and were now sitting in a circle staring at

Taw cum e go qua, who with her high cheekbones and black hair and eyes was very pretty. They touched the beaded embroidery on her dress and moccasins and, had I not stopped them, would have taken the moccasins right off her feet.

When she finished the corn cakes, Taw cum e go qua put down the plate and stood up. Without another word she turned and began walking away from us. "Will you come back sometime?" I called. She didn't answer or even turn around. In a few minutes she had disappeared among the trees.

The work on the cabin went on until it was nearly dark, and another meal was eaten before the last of the wagons left. "Some of these families will not get home until early morning," Mama said. "How kind they were to help us."

"Tomorrow I'll begin fastening shakes onto the roof," Papa said.

"And Libby and I can begin to muddy the chinks," Mama said.

"What does that mean?" I asked.

Mama told me, "There are spaces between the logs where the wind and rain might come in and in winter, the snow. We have to push moss into all the spaces and then cover the moss over with mud."

I was pleased to have some part in building our cabin and began to think of all the places in the woods where I had seen thick green moss growing. Thinking of the woods, I remembered Taw cum e go qua. When I had first heard it, I believed her name a strange one, but now I liked to say it to myself. It was like a small poem. Lying in bed that night, I thought I would like to be friends with the Indian girl, but I did not know where to find her. The Indians did not stay in one place. They would find a good trapping ground near a river or swamp, and when the animals had been caught, they would move on. Even the fields of corn they planted each spring were left on their own to grow. Papa said it took Indians only a few hours to build their houses. I supposed it would be nice to move about whenever you wanted, but I knew I would be glad to have the sturdy walls of the cabin around me when winter came. Although it was a warm summer night, I fell asleep wondering how Taw·cum e go qua would stay warm when the snow began to fall.

VI

When summer went by and no one had asked him to take his compass and survey their land, Papa began to worry. We had little food left and no money to buy more. Mr. LaBelle said Papa might have to cut down our trees and be a farmer.

Papa said he could never do that. Early in the morning and late in the afternoon Papa would walk among the trees. I believe he knew every one of them—how tall they were, how big around, and what birds and animals they sheltered. One tree had an owl's nest. Papa knew because at the bottom of the tree there was fur and bits of bone left over from the owl's supper. In another tree there was a family of flying squirrels. When Papa hit the tree with a wooden stick, the squirrels would come out and glide through the branches.

One morning Papa had to ride to Saginaw, and Mama sent me out to watch over the garden and shoo the rabbits away from the cabbage and winter squash. The garden was close to the pond, and if I was quiet I could see the quick shadows of the little fish beneath the water and, on top of the water, water striders and whirligig bugs. Across the pond the family of ducks was swimming one in front of the other. The ducks were older now, and you could hardly tell the little ones from their mama. I was wondering what it would be like if people grew up that quickly—all in a few weeks—when Taw cum e go qua sat down next to me.

"I didn't hear you," I said, startled. I was glad to see her.

"Why are you sitting here?" she asked.

"I'm watching the garden so the rabbits won't eat our vegetables. We don't have much food for the winter."

Taw cum e go qua always thought for a long time before she spoke, as though out of all the many things she might say, she must pick exactly the right one. "You should plant corn like we do and catch fish and smoke them. Then you would have food for the winter. We catch large fish, sturgeon from the big lake. In the autumn they swim up the river. They are tired then, and the men in our tribe can climb on their backs and ride them like horses. I know many ways to get food."

While I watched, she reached down into the pond and pulled a crayfish out of the water. The crayfish was all white and ugly like a dead hand. I could never have touched it. "There are clams in your pond, and you can find food where the muskrat lives," Taw cum e go qua said.

I had watched the muskrat swim back and forth cutting reeds for his house. "You mean we should eat the reeds?"

"No. But beneath the pile of reeds the muskrat has stored the roots of the pond lily and the cattail. They are good to eat."

"Is it fair to take his food?" I asked.

"Many animals help us find food. In winter we watch for tracks in the snow. The tracks of the squirrels lead us to the acorns they have stored. If we follow the tracks of the deer mouse we find beechnuts."

Just as she always did, Taw-cum e go qua left suddenly, without saying good-bye. Like a quick bird, one minute she was there, the next minute you saw only the empty woods.

When Papa returned, I hurried to tell him how we could find food for the winter.

"I'm afraid we will need more than a few beechnuts and acorns," he said. "I heard today a railroad will be coming through near Saginaw next summer. There will be plenty of work for surveyors then. But we must first find enough food to get through the winter."

Mama had stopped listening to Papa. "Look, Rob," she said. "There are some Indians."

"They must be passing by on their way to their winter camp," Papa said.

"There's Taw cum e go qua's papa," I said. He led the other Indians to us and signaled them to wait while he spoke.

"My daughter tells me you have need for food to carry you through the winter. The blackbirds have been kind this year and we have more corn than we need." He motioned to the men. They put down several baskets filled with corn. There was a gourd of wild honey, and two of the men carried what looked like huge cowhides. "This is mon-e-meg, sturgeon, which we have smoked," he said. "The little fish in your pond are not worth the catching. You must stay well this winter—as well as you made Taw cum e go qua when you cared for her."

Papa and Mama tried to thank the Indians, but such talk embarrassed them and they hurried away into the woods.

It had frightened me to hear our neighbors talk of the cold, cruel winters in this new land, but I had seen so much kindness here that I was no longer afraid.

After we had stored the gifts safely away in our cabin, we all went out to walk among the trees. "This morning," Papa told us, "I found something I want to show you." He pointed high up in one of the elms. I could just make out the nest of a bird, like a little pocket hanging down from a branch. "It's an oriole's nest," he said. "It's empty now. The orioles have gone south."

"Next spring," I asked, "will they be back?" I liked looking ahead to the other side of winter.

"Yes," Papa promised. "Next spring they will surely return."

"And I will draw their picture for you," Mama promised.

About the Author

GLORIA WHELAN is an award-winning author of adult and young adult books. A Michigan native, she researched the stories of the state's early settlers as told in their journals and letters. "One of the stories was of a family who took in an Indian child and nursed the child through an illness," she says. "Later, when the family had little food, the Indians helped them." This story was her inspiration for *Next Spring an Oriole*.

Gloria Whelan lives with her husband in the woods of northern Michigan.